LIVING THROUGH
THEIR DREAMS

LIVING THROUGH
THEIR DREAMS

STEPHAN LUCCAS

THE REGENCY PUBLISHERS

ISBN: 978-1-957724-53-9 (Paperback Edition)
ISBN: 978-1-957724-52-2 (Hardcover Edition)
ISBN: 978-1-957724-54-6 (E-book Edition)

Some characters and events in this book are fictitious. Any similarity to the real persons, living or dead, is coincidental and not intended by the author.

Book Ordering Information

The Regency Publishers, International
 7 Bell Yard London WO2A2JR
info@theregencypublishers.com
https://www.theregencypublishers.international
+44 20 8133 0466

Printed in the United States of America

Chapter One

Growing up was nothing easy, and surely not a bowl of candy and roses. Not to say it was easy for everyone. However, as a child you are naïve to the wonders of this world we call life, always relying on the approval of others. The fear and terror of disapproval is a taste that one comes to know quite instantly, always grasping for some sense of hope, acceptance and acknowledgement.

As a child growing-up in a state of disapproval, Pamela was in self-doubt and feelings that she did not belong. The more she tried to fit in, the more it seemed she felt a sense of being out of place. She was not just an only child, but also a girl. Pamela's parents were good people that only wanted the best out of life for her. Growing up, it became painfully understandable over the years a boy was preferred. Her relationship with her parents were quite temper to some degree because of her gender, as if she was inferior to boys.

Pamela's parents were more of a rough and rumble out going pair, whose belief was to meet life's challenges head-on. In her life, things were tomboyish she remembered. Recalling how she would go out into the back yard with her dad and play, pretending that she was a boxer fighting for the world title. It was all fun at first, because that was when they saw her and she would then exist in their eyes. Pamela's parents were both major lovers of boxing, particularly her mother.

Back in the late 1980's Pamela's mother, Tina back then wanted to be a professional boxer, though at that time it just was not acceptable to be a woman boxer. Instead, she would spend her time going to the gym and watching her friend Sam train and fight, even at times sparring with him. After a while eventually they got married, and shortly thereafter Pamela had been born.

Sam was pretty much what they would call in the boxing world "a club fighter." He was a strong fighter, though he just was not lucky enough to be ranked. He did what he had to do, to put food on the table for him and his bride. However, once Pamela was born everything changed for them both, Sam stopped pursuing his dream of boxing and took on a more stable and consistent line of work.

The first few years were filled with joy and happiness. Not to say they were happy to have a girl, despite the fact that she was a surprise. Her thought was they would have been happier of she was a boy, because a girl now changed everything. That was when their priorities changed as well as, and their focus was became more about providing for their little girl.

As a child growing up Pamela's parents approval was very important, and a strong yearning within her. To the point that she wanted for herself no longer mattered, or it was second best, if at all. Pamela remembered once being asked by her dad, what she wanted to be when she grew up. She looked at his expression of uncertainty upon her face. Taking notice of this Sam told her, "Pamela my dear. You have a strong heart and a beautiful mind, it are these two things that make you who you are and a very special girl." He told her. "So, do not ever let anyone tell you any differently. And, always know I love you."

With baited breath she eagerly asked, "Who's that?" Wanting her him to tell her who she was.

Brushing the hair from across his little girls forehead with an outstretched smile from ear to ear he said, "Anything you want to be, my darling. Because you can do anything you put your mind too."

"I can!" Pamela said with excitement. "What should I be?" She rhetorically asked herself.

Tina with a hopeful tone asked, "What do you want to be when you grow up?"

As a nine year old, Pamela effortlessly said, "Me!"

"Who's that?" Tina asked of her daughter instinctively.

"You," she answered. Pamela could see the tears weld up her mom's eyes, as she then reached out and gave Tina a big tight loving hugged.

As time went on Pamela and her dad continue to play boxing, mostly by her mother's own encouragement. However, who would have ever thought twelve years later she would have gone pro. At age twenty-two, she found it hard to believe. Even now, in these days of the twenty-first century the world was changing, though the road was still quite hard, and filled with its own set of difficult moments. While the world of boxing allowed female boxers, it was not readily supportive in its acceptance. For women boxers everything was more difficult, filled with various challenges. Pamela always had to prove herself, to one degree or another. Nevertheless, like always she preserved.

Things were starting to become more fruitful as her boxing career was on the rise. Pamela began to become more recognizable as those in the boxing world and started taking her more serious, as a true contender. Reached that profession milestone in her boxing career, both Pamela parents were quite proud, more so was her mother, of their daughter. Pamela was quite sure that there would be many more challenges to overcome as her career continued to blossom. However, that was not her concern now, as she was ecstatic with excitement.

Her friends had heard of the wonderful news, they all wanted to take Pamela out to celebrate. Celebrating the fact that she was now a professional boxer, and her first pro-fight. They celebrated hard and drank just as hard.

As the evening festivities went on Pamela had not even noticed that she an admirer. After about he finally approached her and they began to talk the rest of the night away, as she thought to herself how cute, he was. The later and later the night had become, the more loaded, carefree and embolden she became. Ending the night with the taking her newfound friend back to her place. At after some together they eventually fell asleep.

By the next morning, she awoke in bed with a splitting headache, and accompanied by a hangover, from last night. Tossing the covers from across her body, feeling the cool breeze gently kiss her skin, as Pamela hurried to make her way to the bathroom. Just then, as she sat down on the toilet Pamela realized that she was not wearing anything. As she stood at the sink washing the sleep from her eyes, she noticed an image through the reflection of the mirror. Dumbfounded for a minute, Pamela turned around and started making her way back to the bed she was naked herself. Lying beneath her feet, she stumbled across the floor kicking over clothes. Looking down at the different types of clothes Pamela was little confused and still was a bit hazy, but realized that some of the clothes were not hers. Slowly raising her head, she glancing over towards the bed as sense of fear and terror filled her mind and body.

Pamela's eyes widened as she looked upon the body of a naked man in her bed. She thought to herself, 'Oh my god! What have I done?' Unaware of last night's bender she knelt on the bed next to the naked man, and shook his body until he awoke. Then straight away, she started hurling questions at the unknown man. "Who are you? What are you doing here?"

"Stop… Stop…" He said sluggishly, "You're going to make me throw-up."

"Who the hell are you?" Pamela asked, "What is your name?"

Rubbing his eyes he answered, "Tony… My name is Tony. What's yours?"

"What?" Pamela replied in slight disbelief. "What are you doing here in my bed?"

"Really…!" He exclaimed.

"What are you doing here?"

She was not naïve to the current situation now before her, or of the possible events that may have happened last night. However, with a pounding headache, her head was a bit foggy as to what did or did not happen last night. Either way she just wanted to forget about it. "List here Tony, or whatever your name is… Whatever had happened or you think happened last night, it's over with. So get up, get your clothes and go."

"What's your number?" While he begun to get dress.

"I don't give my number out to people I do not know!"

"What's about your e-mail address?"

"No!" Pamela said with an exclamationed tone.

"You knew me well enough last night." He wittingly retorted.

"Well that was last, and it was drunk."

He then asked, "Maybe we can hook up latter?"

"Not a chance." Thoughts race through her mind, as Pamela took a quick once over of his body. As she thought of her boxing career was now on the rise, she did not really want to do anything to jeopardize her chances at further advancement in the sport. "Just get the hell out here."

Without another word, this stranger of the night finished getting his clothes on and left. He did not even try to look back. Quickly throwing on some clothes herself, Pamela rushed out of the apartment making her way to the local pharmacy. She picked up a home pregnancy kit and returned to her place. Heading directly to the bathroom and getting out her pants, she quickly tore open the box and peed on the stick. Anxiously waiting for the results, Pamela set her watches alarm to let her know when the result would be ready. While waiting she did the only thing she could think of, she prayed… Hoping that the results were negative, and she was not pregnant. But what would she do if she were? Pamela had begun telling herself that she just needed to stay calm, as thoughts terror entered her mind.

"What did I do?" She questioned herself. "What was I thinking? How in the world could I something like this? Did I even use any protection?" Fears of concern begun to overwhelm her heart, then the alarm rang out. Pamela jumped, as she was startled. She briefly took a couple rapid breaths and slowly looked at the test strip. Seeing the results, she overjoyed with jubilee that she was not pregnant. From that moment she promised herself for now on it was to be cold showers for her. She began looking towards her next upcoming fight.

Chapter Two

The next morning Pamela went into the gym and begun to train, training harder than she ever had before. Spending time constantly watching videos her upcoming opponent's ring footage. Observing the techniques and style of how her opponent fought, then training on how best to counter it. Pamela trained non-stop for the next five weeks. Then the time had come, and the moment was here.

It was time... The atmosphere in the arena was charged with electricity from the excitement of the crowd. Pamela passed her parents as she made her way to the ring. They shouted out, "We love you sweetie!" At that moment, Pamela felt more alive than ever. Climbing into the ring, all of her senses became acutely and finely a tuned this exact instant. Her vision keenly focused on her opponent directly before her, with a look of determination, letting her know that she was ready to fight. They were evenly matched for the most part, both standing at about five foot-eight inches tall. Pamela herself has long black hair, pulled back in a ponytail; she has brown eyes and a youthful almond like skin tone and physically fit with good muscular definition. Her opponent stood at five foot-nine inches giving her a slight height and reach advantage.

Once the bell rang, both girls immediately came out strong, trading jabs back and forth. They continued that way throughout the first three rounds, and the next several rounds were hard fought, going back and forth. They appeared to be equally skilled round by round, as to the intensity. However, halfway through the seventh round the momentum started shift. Pamela became winded, as she begun struggling in the eighth and ninth round. By the tenth round, every hit from her opponent was unreal, as Pamela's body winced unconsciously in anticipation of the next set of oncoming blows to her body.

Landing repeated blows in the breadbasket, and then two to the face. Pamela's right eye had swollen and her nose was broken. Her legs turned to Jell-O, and with the ringing of the bell the round was over, as the ropes saved Pamela before her body completely collapsed to the matter. Not really satisfied with performance and how the fight ended, Pamela tool the next week, or so, off for a little recovery time. Thinking to herself, what could she have done better? Pamela spent her time reviewing the video of her fight, trying to make since of where she fell short causing her loose the match.

Now feeling fit enough after about a week, Pamela was ready to get back in the gym and get some training done. Pamela then put all focus toward her next fight coming up in the next four-weeks. While she was training Pamela out from the corn of her eye caught a glimpse of her mother, Tina, coming in to the gym.

Keeping her distance Tina sat quiet on a stool in the corner watching her little girl, in action, training with a steely-eyed resolved look upon her face. As Tina could smell the sweat of the bodies in the air, hearing the pounding thudding sounds of the punching bags, and the repeated smacking of the speed-bag. She nostalgically observed her daughter with a warm heart and that of pride. Closing her eyes, Tina's mind fell into thoughts of the past, of how she had herself wanted so much to be a professional boxer.

Finished with her training for the day, not seeing her mother anywhere, Pamela headed straight to the locker room. As she stood in front of her locker, getting undressed, Tina had then walked in standing before her. Taking notice Pamela asked. "What do you want mom?"

In a motherly tone Tina said, "Just to talk with my daughter."

"Well, I'm about get into the shower."

"That's okay," she replied, following her into the show room. While Pamela begun lather up, Tina asked. "How are things going with you?"

After the escapades of the other night, Pamela wasn't sure how to answer that question. "Fine, I suppose."

"You suppose?" Tina responded, "What does that mean?"

Finishing rinsing all the soap off Pamela started dry off, as she and her mom both made their back to her locker. While starting to get dress she asked again, this time with a bit irritation within her voice. "Why are you here mom?" Already knowing what the answer would be.

She answered, "Can't a mother just check in on her daughter, and see how she's doing?"

"Sure, I guess." Pausing for a second, she then said. "Obviously you want to talk. So, what do you want talk about mom?"

"Can't I just want to hang out?" She answered with a smile and continued to say, "And spend some time with my only child?"

Letting out a small chuckle Pamela said, "You spend time with me, don't make me laugh."

"Honestly..."

With a sigh, Pamela relented and said, "Fine. I am going out to get something to eat. Do you want to join me? I'm buying."

"Okay, why not..."

They were having launch outside, sitting in a park, each eating a burger and fries with a cola under a beautifully bright sunny day. They basked in the ray of the sun that broke through the light overcast of clouds, with a slight hint of a cool breeze. Pamela let out a deep exhaling breath said, "Look mom. I know last week's fight was not the greatest..."

Abruptly Tina interrupted her daughter. "That is more than an understatement!"

"What!" Pamela exclaimed, "What the hell do you mean by that?"

In a motherly loving tone Tina explained, "Look here dear. Back when I wanted to be a boxer, things were considerably different. The boxing world did accept women as boxers at that time. Given the chance, I could have been, but I was not even allowed to try. Though here we are in the twenty-first century, and now you have that chance that I did not get." Tina stopped, only for a minute, as she took a bite of her burger and a sip of her soda. She went on and said, "I love you Pamela. I believe you can be this dream of being the world's best female boxer ever, and that is what I want for you. Because of these reasons, I pay close attention not only to your fights, but also to your career. Plus, I can see things you might not."

"All right," Pamela reluctantly acknowledged. "What is it? What is it that you think you see?"

"Like during you last fight, you looked distracted, tired and exhausted. Why is that, are you okay?"

"Mom..." She said defensively. "These are not your run of mill fighters, I am fighting here. They are seasoned girls who can actually fight."

"So you train harder, and fight harder."

No longer, caring for the way the conversation is going; Pamela replied by saying, "Like usual mom you are probably right. I will go back and look at the video. But for now, I have to get back to my apartment and get some rest."

While at the apartment, Pamela was not really able to get any rest, as her mind clung to what her mother had said. Taking notice that she was a bit winded during the last three rounds of the fight. Pamela did agree with one thing her mother that she needed to train harder. By the next morning, Pamela was back in the gym, working out relentlessly. By day's end Pamela was in the ladies restroom puking up her guts, though she was not going to let a little vomiting stop her from training to win. Pamela did not say anything to anyone and continued on fighting. Then four days later, after having some lunch, she threw up again. As a long as there was no blood present, Pamela did not really think much of it.

The puking was about every three or four days. Pamela just figured she needed to eat more, to make for how hard she has been workout lately. As the weeks continued to count down and she really did not care for doctors unless it was a life or death situation. Moreover, there was another fight coming right around the corner. Her training schedule became more intense, harder with shorter rest periods in between. Pamela's idea was to be more focused on her training, as she was not going to let a little stop her. As there was no longer any feeling of fatigue, she continued onward to her next fight.

Focusing on her up and coming fight, Pamela did not even notice the thing around her. The days started to bleed together, leading up to the day of the fight. Before anyone knew it, the event of the day was upon her and it was a night fight. Pamela started the day by getting a hardy breakfast, and then went out for a long peaceful walk. Listening to her MP3 player highly charged blood-pumping music. Pamela's thoughts solely fell into focused on the event and preparation for this evening. She spent the rest of day doing some light cardio, and stretching so to loosen her body and muscles.

As the hours came closer and close to fight time, Pamela went over to her parent's house spending time with them. A ritual she tries to keep is when her fights are in town. They would spend time talking about her boxing career, and their aspiration for the direction of her future. After the lengthy discussion Tina would then say a pray for her daughter panela to be victorious over her opponent.

Usually by the time, they finish their prayer a car would be waiting out front of the house to take them to the where the fight was going to be. Once at the arena, together they would get out of the car and make their way to the security station, where they were by arena escorts and tool Pamela's parents to their reserved seats. Wanting to be close to the action, they would sit in the second row from the ring, something Tina was quite insistent on. Pamela then went straight into her locker room, where she started to get undressed and changed. While getting into her boxing gear, Pamela's mind focused singularly on the task of the nights fight now solely before her.

One of her opponents trainers were present observing Pamela getting her hands wrapped. Next came the boxing gloves, the boxing rob draped over her shoulder and the hoody covering her face. Over the next twenty minutes, she sat on the table in absolute solitude with her own thoughts. Slowly the door then open, and one of the trainers shouted 'it's time.' With that, Pamela's trainer escorted her out of the locker room and down the hall center arena. The crowds' loud roaring was anticipated, and the closer they got to the boxing ring the louder their passion became.

The roar of the crowd begun to fade away as Pamela stepped into the ring and on to the canvas, as she piercingly focused. They both stepped to the center of the ring, as the referee begun to read the rules, and the instructions for the fight. Then they both returned to each of their corns. Then seconds later the sound of the bell rang out, and they both came out swinging in the first round of the fight.

Both fighters stepped out to the center of the ring sizing each other up. They began to swinging at one another, though neither connecting at first. Quickly dropping back on right foot, Pamela snapped forward shooting out several consecutive punches. She then landed one, two, three and four more blows to her opponents face. As if for good measure, two more shot to the women's body.

The opponent answered back with hits of her own to Pamela's face, then to the breadbasket, followed-up with a hard hook to her jaw. Not even fazed, Pamela responded with her own set of punishing hits. The two women went at it back and forth trading blows. In the remaining ninety-seconds, they furiously went at each other. With each punch seemingly connecting harder with even more force then the one before, and the next thing you know the bell rang. Just like that, the battled ended, and the women stepped back to each, not taking their eyes of one another. Now in their prospective corners they continued to stare each other down.

After the bell rung this horrific war resumed between these two women once again. Two minutes into this second round Pamela's opponent lit her up with an unrelenting assault of a flurry of punches to the mid-section and several hook shots to the body. She responded sharply with her own set of shot. Her opponent fired back with some short jabs to Pamela's face again, and then an uppercut to her solar plexus.

Pamela tried to step back, but her opponent continued dart forward unleashing a myriad of punches at her body and face. Falling to the mat doubling over from the forceful uppercut into her gut, causing Pamela to vomit right there on the canvas spewing out blood. Immediately, right there and then, the referee jumped in between the fighters. Waving his arms in the air, ending the fight, and the fight doctor rush into the ring and examine Pamela's condition. Without hesitation, the EMT's hurried into the ring with a stretcher. Still spewing up blood once more, they straightaway rushed her out to the awaiting ambulance. There was the blare of siren accompanied by flashing lights as the ambulance made a non-stop dash to the nearest hospital.

Laying on the gurney in one of the emergency, doctors and nurse check started cutting away Pamela's clothes, as she threw up once again. Her body begun going into convulsion and then stopped once she fell into a state of unconsciousness. While doctors and nurses continued looking over her body, they did stop some vaginal bleeding. One of the doctors immediately ordered an ultra-sound, as they hung a bag of blood and rushed Pamela to the operating room. After the surgery was completed, she was move to ICU where she was lying in a coma for three days. Three days of which her parents spent watching over their little girl, praying and hoping Pamela will some wake up.

During the middle of the night, Pamela had awoken opening her eyes as she started to regain consciousness. Awaking to what appear to be a barren room, she refocused her vision to the dim lighting. Looking around the room she saw fast asleep in a chair at the corner of the room, it was Tom one of her trainers. Anxious to know what happened, Pamela felt the urge to wake him. At that moment, a nurse entered the room to check on her. Taking her blood pressure and pulse, and then asked Pamela some questions.

"So, how are you feeling?" Pamela answered, "Fine... I guess."

The nursed than asked, "Can you tell me where you are?"

"In a hospital," she replied.

"That is good, the nurse said. "Now, can you tell me what happened?"

"I was in the ring getting my bell rung. Then I woke up here in the hospital." Pamela said, and then asked the nurse, "Can you tell me why I am here?"

The nurse than said, "I think it is best that you should ask the doctor when he comes in."

Pausing for a moment, the nurse went on to ask, "Is there anything else you, or I can get for you?"

"No, thank you." Pamela tells her, as she watches the nurse leaves out the room.

Briefly, looking at the trainer, in hope that he could provide some answers, but that turned out not to be the case. Laying there in bed, Pamela turned her head and look out the hospital room window in wonder marveling over what had happened. Thoughts as to the many possibilities began to overwhelm her mind, working her into a frenzy. Pamela became aimlessly entrance by her own thoughts; she had not even noticed that Tom has awoken. She did not even hear at first. Pamela's attention snapped back to the present moment, seeing a familiar and friendly face. Seeing this woeful expression in his face and eyes, Pamela looked back at Tom with a scowl upon her brow, as if to ask what is wrong.

With a gaze of his own, Tom redirected Pamela's attention towards the foot of bed, where at there stood a doctor waiting to speak. Now focusing on the doctor, Pamela spoke. "What up doctor? Did I have a bad burrito, or something?" Everyone let out a little chuckle.

"Well no... It is not anything like that." The doctor promptly replied.

"So then, what happened to me?"

"You got hit pretty hard, and fell to the mat doubling over, and spitting up blood." Tom told her. The fight at that point was ended, and taken out on a stretcher, than you were brought directly here to the hospital."

Looking back at the doctor with confusion and concern, Pamela started to ask questions. "What was the problem? Am I okay?"

In a softer tone the doctor explained, "You suffer some blood lose, and we had to operate."

"What!" She said with trepidation in her voice. "It's okay..." the doctor told her. "The surgery went fine. Now, you'll just need to get some rest and take a bit of a break from things for a while."

Immediately Pamela asked with panic in her voice. "What do you mean I lost some blood?" "You were hemorrhaging when you got to here."

With an exclamation of fear Pamela said, "What?" As a sense of dread came over her, as the visual expression on her face was of utter terror.

"Did you not know?"

"Know what?"

"That you were pregnant," the doctor said. "Your body was hemorrhaging, and you lose a lot of blood. The beating you took caused you to have a miscarriage." As she went on to explain, "We had to perform an emergency hysterectomy... I very sorry, you won't ever be able to have children."

Visibly dejected, Pamela's body collapsed back into the bed feeling her heart fall into the pit of oblivion. There was a stillness that filled the air, as the room became so very quiet you could hear a pin drop. Thoughts again filled her head, as Pamela's mind begun to recall recent past moments of fatigue, moments of puking and increased appetite. With a stun look on her face, Pamela's eyes widened, turning red as they weld up with tears. Tenderly Tom wrapped his arms around Pamela, with an embracing hug of reassurance that everything will be okay. As he, himself, was feeling a sense of hopelessness and lose.

In shock and confusion, she said the first thing that came to mind. "Will I be able fight?"

Taken back for a second by the question the doctor answered, "I don't see why you couldn't." Whit no more questions and after a couple minutes, she left the room.

Later on in the day, Pamela's parent came to see her. Their visit was quite a pleasant but short distraction form the bleak reality of this day. Keeping tight lipped about what the actual problem was she only told them it was some kind of flu bug. Telling them, the doctors just keep her here in the hospital for a couple days observation.

Her parents were concerned with Pamela resting and getting well, though her mother more so, looking forward to her getting back into the box world. Once her parents had gone, and as the day went on, Pamela had become sadden sporadically breaking out into tears.

Unaware of the time a kitchen staff with a tray entered the room presenting her with a dinner. Pamela spent next twenty-five minute starring at her tray, with hardly an appetite. As these menacing thoughts of what the doctor told Pamela, wade on her heart. A little while later, after dinner, a nurse brought with her some medication. Not give any thought as to what she is being given; she took the medication without question. After about an hour or so, Pamela begun to become drowsy and eventually nodded out into a never ending dream world. Tossing and turning most of the night.

By the time Pamela opened her eyes, it was next morning. The doctor stopped to check-in on her, one of the nurses had noted that Pamela had been hysterical, and moment crying throughout the night. Even as she and the doctor were speaking, Pamela had broken down into tears several times. Giving her a moment to regain her composure, the doctor stepped out of the room and made her way to the nurses' station. Writing in Pamela's chart and calling for a psych-evaluation.

Shortly after Pamela had eaten lunch, later in the day another doctor came to visit her. They had started up a conversation, as he began assessing her mental and emotional state.

"Hi!" The doctor said cheerfully, as he asked a couple questions. "How are you doing today?.. Is everything okay with you?"

Without any real thought to the questions Pamela answered with a melancholy like tone, "Fine... I guess."

Following up the doctor said, "Well that's a good thing." He then went on to ask. "How have you been sleeping lately?"

Pamela answered with a gasp, "Not great."

"Why do you think that is?"

"I just have a lot on my mind." Pamela explained. "I just lost a fight, and now I'm laying here in this hospital bed." At that moment, tears begun to well up in her eyes.

Taking a note of Pamela's distress the doctor said, "I heard that we had a b oxer in the hospital. A pretty good one at that, as I understood it." Mindful that Pamela just suffered a miscarriage, and that a traumatic event like this are followed with various levels of postpartum depression. The doctor then explained his and he was to prescribe her some anti-depression medication, and check back in with her over the next couple of days. The name of the medication Pamela is Prozac, and it is at 50mg. twice a day.

A few days alter the doctor return to check on Pamela and see how she is doing. He then asked, "How are you doing today?"

"Good," Pamela cheerfully replied. "So you're feeling a lot better?"

"As good as good can be."

"Well that good to here," the doctor said. As he went on to ask, "How have you been sleeping?"

"Fine," Pamela answered, "Why?"

"I am curious as to if you feel you are getting a good night sleep?"

Pamela went on to say, "Well, I'm sleeping. But..."

The doctor interrupted as he asked, "But what?"

"I'm getting sleep, but when I wake up my body feels restless."

After a minute or so of thought, the doctor told Pamela that would change the medication from Prozac to Paxil at 10mg. once a day. Recommending that she should follow up with a mental-health provider when she is discharge from the hospital. Than shortly thereafter dinner, a nurse entered the room and gave a cup of water a tablet of Paxil to Pamela. An hour later, she fell into a slumberous sleep. Over the next two days, Pamela was discharge from the hospital with the advice to take things slow for a couple weeks, and then see how things are at that point and time.

Chapter Three

Now out, from the hospital, and home staying with her parents as a temporary measure for the moment. At first things were going good, though the sense of restlessness begun creeping in at thoughts of recent events started to fill Pamela's mind. Falling into the wonders thoughts of what if she had not miscarriage. Wondering if she would have kept it? What the baby would of look like, would be a boy or girl?

Reflecting over the many possible baby names it could have had. Contemplating what kind of mother she would have been. Pamela was sure of one thing, that she would not be pushy like her mom. Then thoughts as to the kind of life she would have brought into this world filled her mind, as a strong sense of sadness also filled her heart. However, the pain of lost was so great that Pamela strongly felt it deep down within her soul.

Overwhelmed by this void of emptiness in her chest, Pamela reached out for her medication in hopes that it will numb the pain and calm her nerves. Shortly thereafter, she started to feel a bit better, for a minute. However, after a couple weeks of inactivity of nothingness boredom began to settle in. Tinas unrelenting questioning and nagging of when she is going to get in the ring was becoming too much. Then suddenly Pamela blew her top and shouting at her mother. "Why don't you put a damn lid on it, and just get a life?" She said furiously.

Stunned by her daughters' explosive tone and words anger Tina shouted back. "You are my life!"

Snapping back, she told her mother, "Maybe you should focus more on your own life instead of mine. And, your marriage while you're at it."

With silence gasp her mother answered back, "How dare you!" Tina shouted. "I am your mother little miss thing, and you are my child. Who the hell do you think you are to talk to me that way?" Tears filled her eyes, her voice gave out a sorrowful the tone as Tina said, "Your father and I love you. We only want the best for you."

Seeing the devastation in her mother's eyes as tears rolled down her cheeks, Pamela realized she might have been a bit harsh wither words. Saying, "I'm sorry mom. I didn't mean to upset you, But I am a grown adult, and I have a life of my own to live. Plus, at times, you can a bit much."

Pamela you have skills, and an opportunity to be a champion boxer. Opportunities that neither your father nor I had." Tina went on further to explain. "So; if that means you are mad with me or that you hate me, fine. So be it, I can live with that. But let us be clear on one thing, your father and I would never do anything to hurt you."

"I know mom," said Pamela. Seeing the tears run down her mother face, Pamela let out a sigh as she walked over and put her arms around Tina hugging her tightly. Saying in a compassionate tone, "I know... I know you mean well and you want the best for me. For that, I am grateful. Really, I do truly understand, but for now, I need to get my strength back first. So please, just give it break for now. I've only been out of the hospital of about two weeks.

"I do this because I love you." Tina told her daughter.

Not wanting to prolong this discussion, or burden her mother any more than she already was Pamela just said, "I love you to mom." Sucking up her frustration, she put forth a smile and added, "It'll be okay mom... Everything will be back to normal soon, you'll see." Pamela told her reassuringly.

Pamela realized that eventually she would have get back in to the ring. Therefore, she decided to start doing some light training sooner rather than later would be better than nothing. Pamela began speaking with Rick, one of her trainers. They both agreed to set up a couple light workouts and some sparring matches. After about a month or so, thing seemed to be going good. As they slowly begun to increase her training, after about six months she appeared to be back to full strength as if nothing had ever happened.

The postpartum depression seemed to of resolved itself on its own. In deep thought, self-confidence is exactly what Pamela needs to get back into the ring and finally to move forward with this dream. Becoming one of the world's best female boxers was Pamela's focus. Making a name for herself one, that everyone will be proud of including her mother while writing her own ticket. After another month had passed, Pamela finally was back to her old self as her skills became stronger, her trainers took noticed. Excited at the prospect, they believe she was ready to get back to her career.

Though Pamela first needed to get through a full out physical exam, which she did not think was going to be a big deal. A standard process and protocol after a fight is stop for medical reasons, as it is consider a technical knockout

(TKO). Because of Pamela's recent medical situation and her miscarriage, they had explained to her that they wanted to not only to make sure she was okay physically as well as expressed their concerns for her mental health. So they asked Pamela to undergo a psychologically evaluation. Taken back for a minute by the request, she argued that she was not crazy, and told them no. further explaining that the hospital psychologist prescribed her anti-depressive medication, and they just want to make sure everything is okay. The fact of the matter was that they did not want anyone questioning Pamela's mental stability. After a bit more discussion, Pamela came around, realizing that they were making a lot sense and looking out for her career. They reassured her that the evaluation would be confidential and remain in house, and in the end, their concerns were valid.

A week later Pamela went in for physical, which was standard as physicals' go. She then answered a few health questions and cleared as physically fit. The following week she met up with a psychologist from out of state.

Their conversation started with complimentary platitudes, as Pamela was reserved and careful with her words. As they spoke, her only focus was on getting back into the boxing ring and boxing world again. Eventually after about forty-five minutes the psychiatrist noted that, Pamela appeared to have a little anxiety, but wrote it off as a bit of nerves due to stress at home. Suggesting that she try to relax a little more, otherwise she is fine. Once she left his office, Pamela excited and immediately called her trainers, letting them know the shrink cleared her. Telling them to schedule her for a fight, and didn't care with who. She just wanted things to get back to normal, for whatever that was worth. The psych-eval. Was what everyone had wanted.

Though no one caught on to the fact that there was to Pamela than meets the eye, as she wanted to only get back in the ring.

A few days later Pamela's boxing team had set her up with a fight over next six weeks. It was not anything major, as the idea was for Pamela to get her legs and a couple fights under her belt before going on to the big money makers. Personally, she did not really agree with this plan, but understood their reasoning and just did not say a word. Overall, what she wanted to do is to move on with her boxing career. To just hear the roaring cheers of the crowds as she walked into the ring, with every one's eyes and focus on her.

Pamela's sole focus now is on her training and preparing for her upcoming fight, which was approaching quite rapidly. With two of her trainers, they started reviewing the previous fight style of next opponent. The closer to the day of fight, the harder Pamela trained and the more confident she became. The trainers themselves had also become more confident in her abilities.

Like usual, Pamela spent the day with her parents. The time of the match was getting closer; they all got into an awaiting car together and were on the road to the auditorium. Once they reached the stadium, Pamela went directly to her locker room and begun to get ready. While her parent escorted their reserved seats as usual, in the second row.

Pamela could feel the electrifying charge filling the air, as she made her way through the crowd as she made her way to the ring. It is the sensation that she has so been longing for, that feeling of being a live and of acceptance. Looking over to her right seeing her parents, Pamela looked at them with confidents and a slight smile. Climbing up the box steps to the ring, Pamela stepped through the ropes onto the mat and into the ring. She felt a sense of inevitability, and that of victory. Intently Pamela focused one her opponent with absolute determination, holding a glaring gaze of fiery destruction. The referee recited the rules of the fight, as Pamela look on right through her opponent.

Once the referee had finished they returned to their perspective corners, the bell quickly rang out. Like charging bulls, they went out after one another. Shooting jabs, one after another, with lighting speed alternating from the head to the body. Halfway through the first round Pamela won the fight, with a knockout (K.O.) from a powerful uppercut to her opponents' chin.

Surprised everyone was lost for words in their amazement as to what they had just seen. It appeared as though Pamela had not missed a beat, fighting with a furry. Back in the locker room, there were hugs and cheers of victory, though she just wanted to be alone. Winning by skill is surely sweet she thought to herself. Pamela knew her win was anything but, as she fought out of anger. The next couple of weeks found Pamela struggling over how she had won that fight, as she intensely focused on her training. Then she would her free time afterwards to herself, isolated in her apartment watching the video of that fight night repeatedly. Realizing this she had won with a mixture of skill and anger. This combination scared that scared Pamela, as she could of seriously injured her opponent or worst. Confused as to where this anger had come from and what to do about it Pamela went to speak with her parents and trainers about her concerns. Expressing her thoughts of not fighting for a while until she could figure it out, everyone was clearly unanimous that it was not in her best interest. As they all were quite pleased of the outcome of how her last fight went, their only focus was now towards the fight for Pamela. Explaining that everything would be just fine, and she had another bout coming up in four weeks. It was a surprise to hear as four weeks just right around the corner, and coming up fast.

Pamela while excited and eager, had she own reservations. However, she believing everyone was looking out for her best interest. She pushed forward without any further word. Training and preparing for her next match, Pamela was in the gym working out and sparing. As she struggled against her own thoughts, feelings and concerns as to her life and that of the future to come. Questioning whether boxing was really the life for her. Was it really, what she wanted? Many thoughts filled Pamela's head as fight day approached, and each thought brought a bitter taste of loss and anger.

The day of the fight was no different from usual as Pamela spent the day with parents. It was a day of over cast, as grayish colored clouds filled the sky. With a lingering scent in the air of possible rain to come. Pamela began to get ready as the time creeped up on her. As they started out, her father's cell rang. Answering it as they walked of the house, Pamela took notice of her dad's facial expression. He then told her go ahead and they will see her there.

"Why? What's wrong?" Pamela asked.

Her father said, "One of our friends is in the hospital, and we need to go see him real quickly. Then we will see you at the fight."

"Are you sure?"

"Yah, yah… Don't worry, we'll meet you there like usual." He told her, "Now go before you miss your own fight we'll see you there."

"Alright," Pamela said. She then got into the awaiting car and off the car drove.

Her parents then got into their car and went straight to the hospital.

Arriving at the stadium Pamela made her way directly to the lock room, as begun to mentally preparing herself. Once in the lock room she started to chance, and focused on the task for the night. Walking the through the crowd to the ring Pamela could feel the energy of the crowd, and once again their acceptance of her. The closer they got to the ring; she looked over right shoulder as she started to step into the ring and did not her parents. Not really thinking the worse, she figured they were just a little late.

Chapter Four

Refocusing her attention on the task, as the bell rang. Out both women stepped out to the center of the sizing up each other, dancing around the ring. The first round was slow, ending with no real action. As Pamela went back to corner, she looked out into the crowd to if her parents had shown. However, they seats where still empty. She then turned to one of trainers and asked her parents where, though they had no answer for her. Then the bell rang and round two was on.

Coming out of her corner, Pamela was a bit distracted. Her opponent came out and shot a couple jabs forcing her to fall back stumbling. Pamela regained her footing and got head back by in the game, answering back with her own set of blows. Than both girls went back and forth hitting one another for the rest of the round. By the end of second round Pamela still did not see her parents. Now thoughts of wonder floated through her mind, as now her anxiety turned to anger. As she in part was fighting for them. Then the bell rang out once again and round three begun.

Pamela's opponent darted out on the attack swinging and punching, effectively landing several punishing blows. After a minute, became enraged and answer back with a flurry of pinpoint shot of her own. Bobbing, weaving, and jabbing as she had trained. Hammering away non-stop, this jackhammer like assault was no longer a fight but a brawl. Just a plain old fashion walloping of punishment, a punishment of which Pamela is the sole exacter. Her concussive and relentless pounding collapsed the other girl's face, as she suddenly dropped to the canvas. Seeing her opponent had visible injuries. Pamela raised her arms in victory, as blood dripped off her gloves. The trainers from both corners came rushing into the ring, towards their boxers. The ringside doctor was quickly in along with a stretcher loading the opposing girl on to the stretcher and whisking her away.

In the locker room under the falling water of the shower, Pamela cried out tears in anger and sadness. The reality what had just happened was beginning to set in, that she had let her anger take control. Realizing that she needed to get a handle on her rage, or someone could get seriously hurt. If not killed, something she did not want to be responsible for that. Just after stepping out of the shower Pamela then reached for towel out of her locker, as a trainer of hers entered. Before he could say anything Pamela immediately asked, "How's the other girl doing?"

"She was taken straight to the hospital," he answered.

Pamela then asked, "Has my parents shown up yet?"

The room became quiet as the trainer took a deep breather and told her, "We need to go to the hospital."

"Why?'

"We need to get going right away," he told Pamela. "Don't worry about everything; we will have someone get your thing. But we do need to go now."

Starting to become overwhelmed with anxiety, Pamela begun to worry a little as she then asked, "What's wrong?"

Finally; Mike one of her trainers spoke softly telling her, "Your parents were in an accident."

"What!" she said in shock, "What happened?"

Not answering her, he just said, "Just get dress and let's go. We need to go to the hospital."

Hurriedly Pamela threw on her clothes and they left out without uttering another word. In the car on the way to the hospital, Pamela asked many questions. Questions they could not even begin to answer for her. As they were, only told it was bad and they needed to get to the hospital as quickly as possible. Seeing that Pamela was becoming anxious, Tom one of the other trainers explained that they did not really know much of anything at this point.

The thundering and lighting filled the sky as rain poured down from on this night, quite hard as it was. Pamela's parent had been driving through it on their way to see their daughter fight. Already late, as it was the storm forced them to have to take a number of detours. The fact that the roads were being flooded did not help the matter at all. The down was more than heavy, as the nights visibility was almost nonexistent. Their heads were scanning the road from end to the other, trying to see through the pitch-black darkness of the night to see for other cars. Going down streets not even able to make out any kinds of street-signs, the streets appeared dead, and a kind of void one would imagine in deep space. Crossing deserted intersections and out of nowhere, they were struck head on by a big rig semi.

Now, ten minutes later Pamela and her trainers arrived at the hospital pulling straight up to the emergency doors. Tom and Mike both got out of the car first then helped

Pamela out as they together rushed towards the hospital information desk. Pamela's anxiety again took hold her, as she asked with a sense of urgency where her parents were. A nurse came out from around the desk, escorting all of them to the waiting room. Telling them that she will have someone will be out to speak with them. A short hand for, 'after a while,' Pamela thought to herself. They had been waiting for about two hours before a doctor emerged and spoke directly with Pamela.

As they waited Frank another trainer of hers went down to the hospital cafeteria, to get them all some coffee. While in the cafeteria he noticed a couple of other trainers of the other girl, that Pam fought to night. They had seen him as well. Walking towards each other, they shook hands and made polite chitchat. Discussing why each of them is there at the hospital. Tonight they were no longer competitors on opposite sides. After minutes, they hugged, in support of each, and went their separate ways. Returning with a tray of three black coffees in hand, Frank started to explain that he had just spoken with one of the other girl's trainer in the cafeteria. The girl you fought tonight had died in the ambulance on the way here. Pamela's heart sunk with heaviness, as she was lost for words. Not even missing a beat, she kept her attention focused on why they were here at the hospital. The she walked over to the window and starred out into the night. Standing there, Pamela begun recalling memories of the time she spent with her parents.

Deep in the pit of her stomach, knots came with every passing thought, with it never ending anguish as the knots built on each other. Just as she started to become envelope in every thought, Pamela saw her flection in the glass. Swiftly turning, Pamela began making her way to the center of the room towards the doctor, standing there in his green scrubs. The trainers than got up and stood with Pamela, as she spoke with the doctor. In a consolatory tone, the doctor extended his sympathy as he explained they did all they could, but the damage was too extensive and both her parents passed. Stunned by the sheer shocked and paralyzed, Pamela was unable to make sense of what she was feeling right at the moment. The trainers sat her down into one of the chairs and tried to console her, as Pamela started to hyperventilate. Pamela now was feeling a serve sense of lost, blame and anger all at once. She felt of the night was al her fault. Blaming herself for her opponent's death, whom she had just fought an hour earlier. Then her are now dead, because she didn't insist that they come with her, or that she go with them.

Over the next several days, quite a few of her parent's friends had come to pay their respects, even Pamela's friends had also turn up, out of respect and support. After the funeral, boxing was not really a major priority for Pamela. Getting here parent's things and affairs in order was her focus for now.

Chapter Five

Everyday Pamela would go to the house and inventory her parent's things. Memories of the time spent here with her parents, all of the good and bad, filled her thoughts. Emotions of the past overwhelmed her, emotions of the heart weld up, as tears fell down her cheeks. Thoughts and feelings of regret and sorrow swirled with in her, as everything the she touched held so many vividly intense memories. Bringing their own set of feelings and emotion, each equally tangible as if they taking place at that moment. Time ceased to exist the more enveloped Pamela became in her memories, of what once was. The days started to blur together with an inescapable and sentimental comfort, as days turned too weeks and even months. In the boxing world, it is as if she was not a blip on the screen.

No one had seen or heard a word from Pamela for quite some time, and her trainers begun to worry. With a bad feeling, one of the trainers went to Pamela's apartment, but she was never there. He begun looking around in hopes that here was a spare key hidden somewhere, finding it he entered the apartment. There was an odor of stainless in the air about the apartment, it appeared no had been for quite some time. He then returned to the others and informed them of what he had found. They would make numerus phone calls, just to leave voice mail messages. They would even send her emails and text messages, though still no reply. They then began to wonder if she was staying at her parents place. So they began to make efforts to find the address for Pamela's parents.

For the past three months, no one had seen Pamela, not even by neighbors of her parents. Her friends themselves had not seen her, unless it was absolutely by accident. Pamela would leave her parent's house just to go to the grocery shopping, either in the dead of night or in the early morning hours.

Looking through the file on Pamela and few piece of paper, they found the address for her parents. The next morning Mike and Tom drove across town to the address of Pamela's parents, and once they arrived things did not look to promising. The front lawn was dishevel, the look as if it had not been cute for a while, and the outside of the house looked like it could use of tender loving care. As they went up the walkway to the door, they could smell an indescribable stench in the air. They rang the doorbell, but it did not appear to be working. They then tried knocking, after a minute with no answer. They tried again, this time knowing a little more forcibly. The door then slowly opened, as the odor in the air became more pungent.

"Hi. Does Pamela still live here?" Mike asked, with a smile. Stepping out from the shadow into the light Pamela said, "It's me." As she extended her, arms reaching out to give each of them a huge hugging embrace, of longing.

At first, they did not recognize her, because Pamela looked different. Looking nothing like the person, she once was. Appearing to of ages, thinner than before and wasted.

She had lost a lot of weight, as her eyes blood shot red and her hair tattered. Pamela asks, "What bring you all the way out here? With the smell of alcohol on her breath.

"We want to see how you were doing," they said with clear concern in their voices. "We had not heard from you for quite some time, and we were worried," said Tom.

"Well here I am, and doing fine." Half heartily, Pamela told them.

"That's good to hear." Mike asked, "Can we come in?"

"Of course... Do come in. But please pardon the mess; I'm still trying to straighten things up." Pamela then told them, "Things are just a little bit longer than I original thought."

Seeing several empty boxes lying around as they entered and walked through the house, things appeared in obvious disarray. Making their way to the kitchen, the sink filled with dirty dishes and half-eaten food on the counter. The microwave did not work, and nor did the refrigerator. As Mike opened the icebox, they were hit an overpowering smell and sight of spoiling food. Seeing the over following trash spilling onto the floor, as well several empty liquor bottles laying around the kitchen and on the kitchen table.

"What's wrong with microwave, and icebox?" Mike asked.

"Oh, nothing."

"It doesn't look like nothing." Tom inter jested.

Pamela told them, "The power company just turned it off recently."

"When was that?" Mike clearly asked with shock and concern in his voice.

"Oh, it's nothing. I just haven't got around to getting it turned back on." She retorted.

Tom asked, "How long has power been turned off?"

"I'm really sue," Pamela answered, "I think it's been about five or six weeks."

"What!"

It is okay, it has helps me to save some money," she said.

"What about the food?" "Waste not, wants not my mom always use to say," Pamela said.

Feeling uneasy about Pamela's situation and her answers, Tom and Mike stayed a little while and a bit more with Pamela. They spoke for almost another two hours before Mike and Tom had to go, and start making their way back to the gym. During the drive Tom and Mike started discussing what they had just witness and their concerns. Both shared the feeling that something was seriously wrong. Once back at the gym they went upstairs straight away. Entering the office, they began to explain to Frank, the head train and owner of the boxing gym, what they seen and their concerns, and their opinion about it. They tried to figure out what to do, and how best to help Pamela.

As Pamela was a very stubborn and headstrong individual, and strong will fighter. Which meant helping her was not going to be easy. The change in her appearance was a distracted one to say the lease, as her face held a clear look of pain and surrender.

After some further discuss, for the past three days, of what to do they all went together to speak with Pamela. However, this time they brought with them a psychologist, to help assess the situation. Once they arrive at Pamela's parent home Pamela greeted them at the door, as she invited them in. The psychologist, thirty minutes into their visit, bean to talk more directly to Pamela. Expressing every ones concerns, and asked how she was doing. Her response was somewhat sluggish and disoriented. Concerned the psychologist pressed on, asking few more questions. "How are you feeling today?"

"Honestly," Pamela answered, "I am a bit tired."

"Why do you that is?" The psychologist asked.

Pamela replied, "I'm just been really busy with packing up all my parent's things."

"I understand you parents had just passed away."

"Yeah..."

"How long ago was that?"

"Not long," she said.

Seeing all the various different liquor bottles lying around the psychologist asked, "How are you dealing with it?"

Pamela said, "I'm doing fine."

"Were you parents' heavy drinkers?"

"Are you drinking?"

"Just a little from time to time," said Pamela.

The psychologist then asked, "Are you sure you're okay?"

"Of course, I'm all good." She retorted.

Not really believing Pamela, and had noticing of some pills openly lying around, the psychologist became concerned and encouraged her in getting some help. Seeing she was not receptive to the suggestion, they ended their visit. Tom told Pamela they would call her later. A week later Mike and Tom returned back to Pamela again let her know their feelings, explaining that they feel she needed some serious help. She laughed at the thought that there was something wrong, as she sipped her glass of JB. They then argued back and forth for few minutes, and then she came to realize that they really were concerned about. To settle every ones worries, if nothing else, Pamela finally agreed to check herself voluntarily into a local rehab facility.

The first couple of months focused around her alcohol and prescription drug use. Pamela at first did not eating much and spending most her time isolating in her room. Depressed and crying herself to sleep, feeling the she had failed everyone letting them down. Eventually she came around eating and started to socialize with the other residents. Over the next few months, Pamela started to open up, and discuss the issue of her pain. She was becoming more engage in wanting to understand the cause for this conflict within her.

Now personally, Pamela had begun to gain a better sense of awareness as she continued onward in taking her daily meditation class. This realization of awareness filled her with a strong sense of balance and harmony. An energy that was similar to what she felt when she was in the ring, but more. It was a calming balance within from within, and a loving sense of acceptance.

To understand better this newfound inner peace, Pamela began to keep a journal of her meditational experiences she periodically read over her written entries. While realizing some self-evident facts, about herself and, of her life, such as the life she was living was not hers. But that of her parents. Though upon further refection, she became aware that her chosen career was more her mother's dream, than hers. And, Pamela's mother was more insistent then her father was. He had always wanted was her to happy in whatever she did. Back then, Pamela was quite compliant, trusting her parents had her best interest at heart. Like any other child longing for approval and to make them proud. As Pamela did as well, at lease that was the reasoning.

It was the reason why Pamela never said anything about her miscarriage. Not wanting to burden and disappointing her parents, especially her mother. Causing an already strained relationship to become even more strain, and fill with event more difficulties than it already is. She recalled her mother's word. "Life is a series of choices that you can cause to happen, Choices which you and you alone are solely responsible for. So that no one to blame, but yourself" To a child those words were quite profound and intimidating. As a kid and even now, as an adult Pamela take s those words to heart and living by them. Holding herself at fault for her parent's death, believing that she could have done something to of prevented the accident itself.

Though threw continued meditation, journaling and therapy Pamela slowly reached a point of stability and self-awareness. No longer was she blaming herself, or trying to obtain the approval of others to live her own life. Pamela came to understand that not every choice always works out the way we think or want them too. They are neither good nor bad, they just are. Like another chapter in a book and the turning of a page. Pamela's realization here made it easier for her to accept herself Feeling a level of perseverance in the belief success and happiness that still yet to come was her way.

Now this new sense and need with in Pamela to move forward with her life was a strong desire within. Not sure, what the future may hold for her, Pamela was sure about one thing. That one thing was clearly that boxing was not it. So, she spent the next several weeks before her discharge in though and wonder of what this chapter would bring. With a bit of fear as to the many possibilities of starting a new page in this journey called life.

Chapter Six

The day of discharge finally had arrived as Pamela left out the program full of self-pride and reassured of who she is, ready to move forward with a new part of her life.

Out front, there was an awaiting cab, which Pamela entered with some uncertainties as to what next to come, as the cab drove away. Heading directly to the boxing gym where she once trained, thinking it would be better get this over and done sooner than later. As wonders filled her thoughts, as to how they would react to seeing her again. How they would take news? Pamela acknowledged that this would be a big step for her, and for everyone that helped to support her.

Just then the cab pulled up in front of the gym, Pamela looked up at the building with some hesitation in her heart. Though in her mend she knew this was the right thing to do. Opened the door, and Pamela slowly stepped out of the cab. Turning around Pamela just stood there in front of the gym entrance still feeling a little bit of hesitations and unsure, but with a deep breath, she stepped through the double-doors into the gym. As the locker room smell of body sweat and dirty socks filled her noise, stirring past memories of her time when she would come in to get her work out on.

Persevering Pamela continued walking through the gym and was greeted by some of the other trainers, as she made her way to Frank's office. Pausing at the foot of stairs, as she turned back to look out over the gym and remembered some of the good times she had had. At that moment, a little sadness washed over her. Turning back to the stairs she to make her way up and entered Frank's office.

As door opened Mike, Tom and Frank greeted Pamela with hugs of joy to see her again. Reminiscing over what once was, they spent the next hour talking. Frank asked, "So, how you been feeling lately?"

Answering Pamela said, "Honestly, quite well."

"What about mow?" Frank followed up.

"Look, over all I am doing pretty well." She had told him. "But a little edgy at the moment."

Hearing what Pamela had said, Frank chose to press on. "Well, that's great to hear," he said with enthusiasm. "What's your plan for the future?"

"I'm not really sure at the moment," Pamela said.

Tom piped in and asked Pamela, "Have you taking care of yourself?"

"Yah... Of course I have."

"Really," Tom retorted.

Pamela at this point began to explain, "Look guys. Okay, I have kept up with training to box. But while I was in treatment I had a lot of time to do some reflection, and came some realizations." Pausing for a minute to get her thoughts together and breathe. She went on to say, "First; I want to say thank you for all you have done. Thank you for caring about me."

"You're our girl," said Mike.

"Really," Pamela asked with a look of wonder upon her face.

"Of course you are..." Frank replied with no reservation.

"Then that makes what I have to say even more difficult," Pamela, says.

"Whatever it is, we can work through it." Tom says, not knowing exactly what Pamela was about to say. Telling her it will all be okay.

"Well, I had a lot of time to think and consider some of the life choices I've made over the years."

"Okay, we are listening." Mikes voice dragged on. "What are you trying to say?" As Mike was a more direct type.

"I am leaving boxing."

Surprised, disbelief was visible in his eyes as he said, "But you love boxing."

"Yes, Tom. I do love the sport, and I always will. However, it was never my dream."

"So, whose dream was it then?" Mike chimed in.

Pamela then said, "Well, to be honest. It was my mothers, and I want her to be proud of me. I stayed in it in the hopes things would change but then I became pro. Though not to rehash everything, I love boxing but I am in love with boxing."

Listens to what Pamela was saying, Frank listened intently in silence. This was nothing that he has not encountered before in his thirty years as a trainer. Tom just stood there looking at Pamela indifferently, for a couple minutes, letting out a light sigh as if of disapproval. Shaking his head as he made a straightway too and out the door, leaving the office. It obvious Tom did agree with Pamela's decision, but it her decision.

On the other hand, all at the same time Mike was supportive, and a little sadden. Over the years, he and Pamela became friends and quite close. Mike did not know if this was the best choice for her, and it was her choice. Mike just wanted her to be happy. Reaching out he gave Pamela hug, and said. "Girl you do what makes you happy, and I'll be there for you." With that, he turned and left out the office.

Now leaving Frank and Pamela the only two in the office, as Pamela sat in the one of the chairs before Frank's desk and they began to talk. Wanting to explain herself, Pamela said. "I don't want you to think I'm a quitter here."

"Oh, Pamela... My dear that is the furthest thought from my mind, that is where your concern." Frank told her.

"It is?"

"Yap..."

"Why's that?"

"Because for anyone to be in this business they have to be a fighter, no matter what their reason." Frank told her, "And Pamela you are definitely a fighter, in more ways than one."

"Well, thank you for the compliment."

"It's not just a compliment. It the hard cold facts," Frank answered back.

"I don't know what to say." Pamela said all chocked up.

Standing up from behind his desk Frank walked around to the front, next to Pamela leaning the edge of the front the of the desk. Frank then leaned over, as Pamela looked upward at into his face. "Darling, this is your life. A life made of choices, choices of how we want to live your life.

However, these choices require a level of strength we all must find within ourselves." As Frank paused for a breath Pamela a rose from her seat. Now, eye to eye, Frank smiled as he put his hands on Pamela's shoulders as he told her. "That being said, I believe in you and that you'll succeed whatever life has in store for you." He gave her a firm fatherly hug, and watched as Pamela walk out the office.

Just as Pamela closed the door behind her, she quickly went down the stair and through the gym. Not stopping bushing through the old smell of a now past life, out the building. Smelling the fresh air, that is city air. For Pamela it is the smell of newness, as she got ready to go forward into the charted unknown.

Standing before the door of her apartment, Pamela paused with a sense of joy to be home. Turning the key and opening the door Pamela stepped into the apartment, feeling a weight fall from her shoulders. See the door to her room opened a jarred, thoughts of sleeping in her own bed filled her heart. After a year of sleeping in a strange and unconformable bed, she now is ready to lie in her own bed. Overwhelmed with personal joy from the idea finally to sleep in her own room and bed. Stepping toward the bed, Pamela went ahead and sat on the edge. Feeling the relaxing confront under her butt, the rest of her body fell back on to the bed. Closing her eyes only for a minute was all it took, as Pamela lazily drifted off into a restful slumber for the rest of day.

A waking by the next morning, Pamela got out the clothes she was wearing from yesterday and then stepped into the shower. Washing away the grime of the previous day, stepping out to a kitchen so to make herself a cup of instant coffee. She moved to the couch, gently sitting down and leaning back sipping her coffee. Letting thoughts freely flow her mind, thoughts of what to do now. However, for the moment Pamela's only concern was what to have for breakfast? Was she going to make breakfast, or go out? Thinking 'that if she was to go out than she would have to get dress.' After about thirty minutes of relaxing and finishing her coffee, Pamela decided that she was going out for breakfast.

Finally, Pamela raised her butt off the couch as stood up, going to the kitchen and made herself another cup of coffee. Sipping her cup of Joe, she walked back to her room to get dress. Throwing on a pair of sweat pants, an A-shirt and a pair of sunglasses as went out the door. Wanting to enjoy the air and clear the cobwebs from her head, Pamela decided to take a jog instead of driving. Plus, it was a chance for her to get some exercise and cardio for the day.

As she took her morning run, for breakfast, she felt free once again. Smelling the city air and hearing the traffic about, feeling the warmth of the sun's rays upon on her skin. As she was enjoying her run, she started forgetting everything that had past, her thoughts begun to look towards the future. After two miles of running, Pamela caught a McDonalds and decided to go in and grab something to eat there.

As Pamela went in, she stood in line, and as she waited, her turn thoughts filled her mind. Then she was call up to the counter, as she placed her breakfast order and tall coffee. Once getting her order, she went to a table and sat down. Pamela sat there eating and drinking her coffee while stared out the window into the city skyline, her mind filled with many wonders of possibilities. She was preoccupied with questions as to what to do now. Considering that, there where overwhelming choices in which to choose from, and just then Pamela realized that she had never really given it any thought. Nevertheless, for the moment there was not any real hurry to make a decision right this minute today. Finishing, her breakfast she went up to counter and ordered another cup of coffee to go. With something in her now, Pamela decided to walk back home. The walk itself gave her a chance to ponder what was to come next in life.

By the time, Pamela made it back to her place, as she realized that she a loner had an income from boxing. Nor could she sustain living in her apartment and her parent's home. For a couple weeks she struggled with what to do, there only three more months left on her apartment lease and had not decided what to do. Looking at her bank statement Pamela quickly became aware that her little saving was dwindling. As much as she wanted her own house, Pamela knew that she could not live there. Therefore, she decided to put it on the market, and a few weeks she got an offer. After getting the money in her bank account, her next step was to decide whether to renew her lease, or not.

Chapter Seven

Pamela started seriously consider what she wanted to do with her life going forward from this point. Boxing had given Pamela the opportunity to travel and see different places, and she thought about traveling again.

If traveling is going to be a possibility, as there where some questions that first needed to be answer. Such as where to go, and how much it would cost? What would be the best away to travel? However, before all that, she needed to figure out how she was going to support herself financially. These were all good questions, though Pamela herself really was not sure. After about a week, she started to figure things out. Realizing that however she decided to go about her new travels, everything to sustainable.

Therefore, Pamela first started with checking what was in her bank account to see what she current had to work with. She then begun to the newspaper for a used truck campers, but that is road and travel worthy. Finding a few different one for sale by private owners meant she would be able to possible wheeling and dealing. Pamela made several phone calls and set up times to go check them out. Once seeing five different camper trucks, Pamela settled on one. Next insurance and what it was going cost. Since Pamela the camper trucks was going to be her new home for quite a while, she went ahead and got full coverage.

To cut her expenses and have some extra cash to get a few other things, Pamela started to sell a few things. Selling all of furniture, dishes, linen not want leave have and bills for the cost of storage. Pamela also sold most of her clothes, as she was downsizing. She also put her parent's house on the market, getting a hefty penny for it. Excited, and with only three weeks left on her apartment lease Pamela went to her apartment manager. After explaining her situation, the apartment manager agreed, let her out of her lease and even allowing her to keep her security deposit.

By early the next morning Pamela had everything packed up and ready to go, she just had to return the key the managers' office.

Enthusiastic Pamela took a deep breath as turned the key in the ignition. With wonder in her mind, Pamela pulled out of the apartment parking lot on to the road. Driving passed her old gym fond memories flashed through mind, though she continued toward the freeway. Sitting at an intersection waiting on the light to change, Pamela was feeling a little hungry. The light had turned green and as drove down the road, pulling into a local Mexican drive-through. Not to stop again for something to eat Pamela ordering two large breakfast burritos, saving one of them for later and a large coke.

Then from there she drove across the street over to the gas station. One finishing filling up her gas tank she went in to pay. While in there she also purchase a map of the country, then went back the truck and pulled away from gas pumps and parked off to the side. Starting open the map and begun to one of the burritos. Sipping on her soda,

Pamela started to open the map to see which direction she wanted to start her travels. Looking at the many different routes to take she really was not sure. However, after finishing the burrito and her coke she had made decision. Pulling out of gas station heading towards the 1-17, and got the freeway going north up to 1-40. Only stopping outside of Prescott to get some more gas, stretching her legs and go use the restroom. Then it was back the road again.

Leaving Phoenix Pamela roll the window down hanging her hand slightly out the window, feeling the cool air breezing through her fingers. Feeling a surge of energy pulsate with in her body, as excitement of was to come. Thoughts of wonder filled her as to who she was, or could now be. Now there was no one telling her who or should be, thinking I am free. Responsible for what she does next and she chooses to live her life. As she reached, Flagstaff Pamela decided to take detour to see Sunset creator. Driving along the road to the top, she took notice of volcanic rocks. Pulling off to the side, she got out and collected some of the rocks, and putt them her camper, as talking pieces and paperweights. Back in the truck, she started the engine and turned around heading back down.

Pamela then went on to see a place she only been told about, but she always was focus on her training. Now Pamela did not have anything stopping her exploring interest this time. So she went to one of Arizona's recognize state land marks, one of the world's most important places. This place of wonder was the Lowell Observatory, which was founded by the astronomer Percival Lowell back in 1894. However, nowadays it operates several different telescopes carrying out a wide range of research.

Paying the entrance fee, Pamela went on to explore the observatory. Breaking away from the tour group, she stepped off the beaten path. After a while, Pamela came upon a round building, and as she walked closer, as she went up the steps she could read the plaque be for the building. Looking through a window as she pressed a button and a light come on, seeing the actual telescope Percival Lowell observed stars through. The energy of excitement and intrigue began to fill her mind as her skin got goose bumps. What a sensation Pamela thought to herself. Then she heard a voice say, "It look amazing, doesn't?"

"Yes," Pamela retorted in one word.

"Are you authorized to be here?" Not who this person is Pamela said, "Yes."

"That's funny, because I work here and I've never see you around here."

Realizing she was caught Pamela explained, "Look obviously I don't work here, and you that. I just want the real stuff, not the bull shit crap of new things. The historical things, the real articles you can understand that. Can't you?"

Pausing to take a moment he said, "Look I can understand your enthusiasm but you cannot really be here so far away from the tour group. So, let us go ahead get you back to them. And maybe you'll want to check out the Giavale open deck observatory."

With Pamela to her leave as she took notice of the wonders around her, making it straight out to her truck. As she got in behind the wheel, she was the other burrito. Staring the engine Pamela got back on the highway, taking 1-40 going eastward while eating the burrito. Crossing the four corners as the day light began to settle behind her. While driving through the New Mexico night, Pamela could not help but out up towards the stars considering the many possibilities of the worlds out there. Pulling into the area, Pamela parked and got into to her camper to some coffee. Then stepping back out and sitting down in the doorway of the camper, Pamela sipped her coffee. Looing upon its wondrous beauty, she gazed into the night sky.

Her filled with the many questions of wonder? Asking herself, are we the only ones in existence? How many different worlds are out there? What do they look like, how they live?

As the night grew later, exhaustion overwhelmed her mind and body. Pamela's eyelids became heavier with every blink. Making the decision, she climbed into the camper and locked the door behind her. Kicking off her shoes, she stretched out and fell into a fast slumber for the night. Awaking the next morning from a restful sleep went out to the public restrooms, then brushed her teeth, put on some deodorant, washed her face and brushed her hair. Back in the camper, Pamela changed clothes, getting into a pair shorts, a t-shirt with no sleeves and a pair of flip-flops.

Back in the driver seat, she got going down the highway, looking for a truck stop to get some gas and something to eat. About fifteen mile later down the road just over the Texas state line was a little town. Getting off the highway, she first went to get gas. With the tank full, it was now time to get something to eat. The question was where. About half a mile behind the gas station Pamela saw a Waffle House, figuring that a good of place as any to get some breakfast and drove over to there.

Business for the morning appeared a bit slow, at lease for this morning. Seeing that booths were opened Pamela walked over and sat in one of them that next to where the action is. Close to where the food is being prepared. A waitress and took her order. Pamela ordered the all you can eat breakfast, starting with a cup of coffee, two eggs sunny side up, hash brown and bowl of grits with honey. The smell of the being prepared gave her sense of confront. Once finished preparing her breakfast, the cook delivered the plates over the partition to her table.

Sipping a her coffee Pamela dug into her eggs and hash browns as she began thinking about what she was do keep money into her bank account so to fund travels. She something she could do while letting her continue to keep mobile. Putting butter and honey on her grits continued to consider the many different possibilities, Pamela ordered another cup of coffee and stared out the window of restaurant. Watching the morning sun come up from the east, an idea finally came to mind. She wanted to be something that she would enjoy doing.

Finishing breakfast, she paid the bill and went out to the truck.

Pamela then made her way over to a Wal-Mart down further down the road in town. Active was slow for the morning, making it easier find what she was looking for. Ending up in the computer department, where Pamela purchased herself a laptop and camera for the laptop and internet. Then she headed over to camera department of the store, picking a telescope. With everything in hand and paid for, Pamela went straight out to the truck, putting the telescope in the camper Taking laptop with her to the cab of the truck.

Pamela's idea was to do a continuous running blog of her travels. Once she setting up her blogging account, she was back on the highway again. She drove through the upper part of Texas, then into Arkansas. Driving down the interstate, it was in a magnificent, as there stood beautiful fifty-foot richly green trees on either side. Stopping in Little Rock to get some gas and restock on her supplies.

Pamela than pulled the laptop and began to blog, typing out freely her thoughts. "Well hay there everyone, my name is Pamela and this is my traveling blog. My travels started out of Phoenix, Arizona.

Now Phoenix is a nice city, for being in the middle of a dessert. However, it was getting too big at lease for me. Moreover, after spending the majority of my life there it was time for me to grow beyond the state boarders. Now look at me, here I am three states, here I am blogging.

I also got me a telescope so I see what is out there beyond out world. Actually, I got the idea after visiting an observatory back in Flagstaff. I had become so inspired, so I decided to get me a telescope and see the stars. While sharing my thoughts with world, at lease those willing to listen to my rambling.

So, while you all think about that I will sign off and blog at my next stop. Until than always remember, you can do anything you put your mind too." Pamela then got back on the road.

Continuing to move eastward with no real plan as to what do next, Pamela just drove. Only pulling into various rest stops for the call of nature, and so she could sleep for the night. Awaking the next morning to a whole new day, in wonder as to what it would bring. Driving for most of the morning, Pamela crossed state lines into Tennessee then into truck stop. As she went in to the restaurant, she notice of what looked like a gift shop and laundry map all rolled in one. Walking up the counter she sat in one of the stools, and ordered cup of coffee. Grabbing one of the menus and reading over her options to eat. However, only 10 o'clock in the morning, they were still serving breakfast. Lucky for Pamela, she was craving some waffles and orange juice. The waitress came and took her order. Pamela asked for a Belgian Waffle and orange juice. The waitress asked, "What kind of syrup would you like?"

Queries' Pamela asked, "What do you have?"

"We have maple, strawberry, blueberry and blackberry syrup. Which would you like?"

"I think will try blackberry syrup."

"Would you also like some honey butter to go with that?"

Realizing she heard of honey butter let alone had it she said, "Sure, thank you. And if I may, can I get another cup of coffee."

While waiting for her order Pamela let the waitress, know she was going check out gift shop. With coffee in hand, she made her way over to the gift shop/laundry map. As she thought to herself after she finished her breakfast, she could get her clothes washed. Back at the counter, she sees her food was there and ready. As she sat at the counter eating, Pamela got hold of the waitress and inquired if there was a place she get a shower. The waitress explained that they had showers, but they are pay shower rooms.

It was a one-person stall with two hooks on the wall, for hanging your clothes and towel. Being that was used to taking in an open bay, she did not have an issue with it. However, she did have a little trepidation, being it was in such public area. Thinking it would be a new and unique experience. Once finishing food, Pamela went out to the camper, got a change of clothes, and secured a heavy solid door behind her, as she begun undress. It was a shorter shower than Pamela is use to, as the water turned off after only ten minute. Nevertheless, this was new way of living, she thought to herself as she wiped the soap from her eyes and under arms. Dried off and dressed she step out from the shower with her hair still a bit wet. As Pamela made hastily march out to her truck.

Pamela than gathered the rest of her clothes to be wash, and then the laptop from the cab of the truck. After getting her laundry going Pamela started blogging. While still trying to figure out what she wanted to with her life. Once she moved her clothes from the washer to the drier, she went to get herself some coffee and waiting for her clothes to finish drying. There was a T.V. in the laundry mat, turn on some stock program. Talking about day traders, and how the whole process of trading worked. It seem interesting enough she thought. Sitting back sipping her coffee, Pamela open the laptop and started to blog.

"Today I am sitting here drinking my coffee and doing my laundry. I caught this program on T.V. about trading stocks, and how people that day trade effect the price of a company and the economy. That surely one way to make some cash.

I am more concern with keeping myself a float and fed. I'm sure you all out there would agree. It looks like my clothes are dry, so end the blog for now. I will talk to you all later."

While folding her clothes Pamela found herself thinking about she get started with as a possible income. As put her clothes away and started her drive down the highway. Wondering how much money she actually make and would need to get started. The more thought she put into the idea the more it sounded like a good idea.

Night was approaching as Pamela drove towards the dawn of her new future.